I Like to Read!

by Miriam Sklar

ISBN: 978-1-338-75077-5
Illustrated by John Lund

Published by Scholastic Inc., 557 Broadway, New York, NY 10012

10 9 8 7 6 5 4 68 25 26 27/0

Printed in Jiaxing, China. First printing, January 2021.

I read in the store.

I read in the drawer.

I read in the park.

I read in the dark.

I read in the bath.

I read in the grass.

I read in your lap!